MW00873130

The only
Gift
is a portion
of thyself.
·Ralph Waldo Emerson·

Eliza has a Cousin

·ISBN 978-0-9853223-5-9·

Rose Water Cottage
·Press·

·story·illustrations·calligraphy·····
···Christie Jones Ray··

Grammy's House Books
A Mouse-Making Guide
Eliza... the Mouse in Grammy's House
Eliza and a Cottage Door
Eliza has a Cousin
Pick-a-Pick-a-Pumpkin
The Fox Family of Franklin

This book is dedicated to our Tia,
mother of "the little boy who comes
to visit", for bestowing me with the
name Grammy...
...And in loving memory of her
mother Nancy Gail Moss Ray
1960 ~ 2003 ~
...who hand~spun the wool, the
color of mushrooms, and hand~
dyed the wool, the color

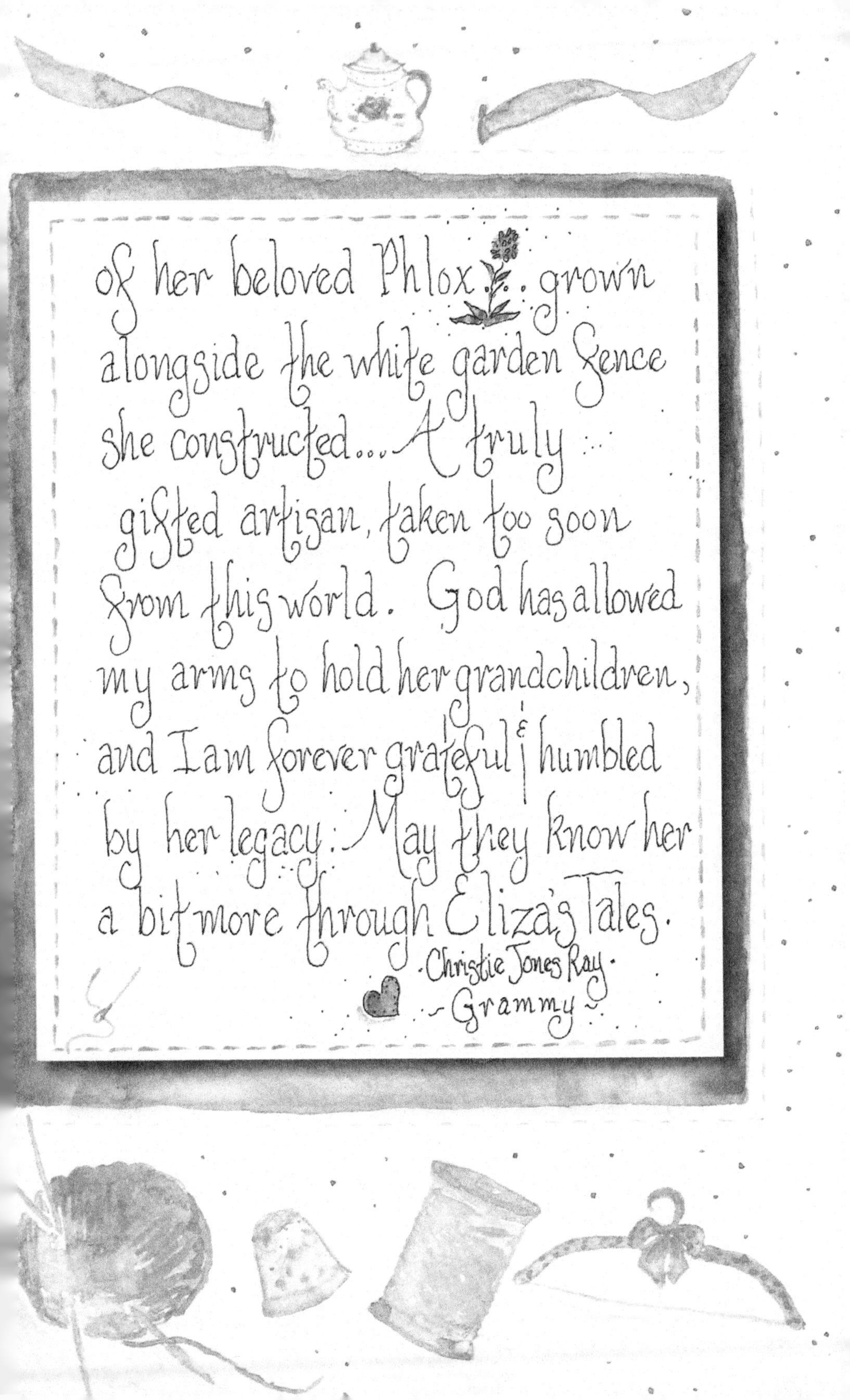

of her beloved Phlox . . grown
alongside the white garden fence
she constructed... A truly
gifted artisan, taken too soon
from this world. God has allowed
my arms to hold her grandchildren,
and I am forever grateful & humbled
by her legacy. May they know her
a bit more through Eliza's Tales.

·Christie Jones Ray·
~Grammy~

Wherein Eliza learns of cousin
City Mouse
Eliza, the sweet country mouse, discovers she has a cousin, City Mouse, who lives quite far away
and enjoys tea parties on very special occasions.

Curiosity
overwhelms our dear
Eliza, and she inquires
of Grammy what
wardrobe
might the cousin have in her
home in the city.
Mouse Slippers Size: .007
Chapeau

"Her closet is bare...
...Cousin is a
newly stitched mouse,
as well, and in need
of an everyday
shawl,"
replies Grammy,
"for those chilly spring days."

Eliza asks her
mistress might she
knit one more very
fine shawl with
Hydrangea
blue ribbons... that heavenly hue.

Yes, indeed.
A shawl of fine
hand-spun wool...
the color of
mushrooms
found deep in the woods...
would be knitted with tiny
needles.

City Mouse enjoys delightful tea parties, so it is decided that she should have a pretty pink shawl of hand~dyed wool.
Jam

The shade is
the very color of
Phlox, a tall flower
that blooms late
in the spring
and throughout the summer.

In her sewing basket filled with notions, Grammy finds a length of hand-dyed ribbon bearing the name 'Blossom.'

It is quite lovely attached to the knitted tea party shawl.

And most
certainly, her
wardrobe would not
be complete
without a
kerchief.
·a scarf worn about the neck·

A tiny
remnant remains
of Grammy's loved~
off bit of hanky.
The heavenly
blue ribbon is sewn on the tips
of the tiny new
scarf.

The sweet wardrobe is ready.

A teeny tiny
box is found for
the teeny tiny
wardrobe going
to one
very sweet cousin who lives
far away in the city.

Country House
City House

The handmade gifts are wrapped in pink tissue paper and carefully tucked in the tiny box.

The small package is set aside, as more treasures are prepared.

U.S. MAIL
U.S. Mail
All shall be going by post and they must reach her in time, for a very special event fast approaches
The Globe News
ROYAL WEDDING

Eliza whispers to John Jacob
"She will be
so surprised."
John Jacob whispers to
Eliza, "She mustn't
squeak too loud...
for Matilda the cat might
POUNCE!"

Yes, City Mouse must
always
watch for the cat, as
John Jacob has
learned he must
always
watch for Scout the Yorkie
who once snatched him away.

Mistress Grammy
will take
much more care
to watch over
her tiny
residents
here in the country house.

CPSIA information can be obtained
at www.ICGtesting.com
Printed in the USA
BVOW07s0743190317
478865BV00008B/577/P